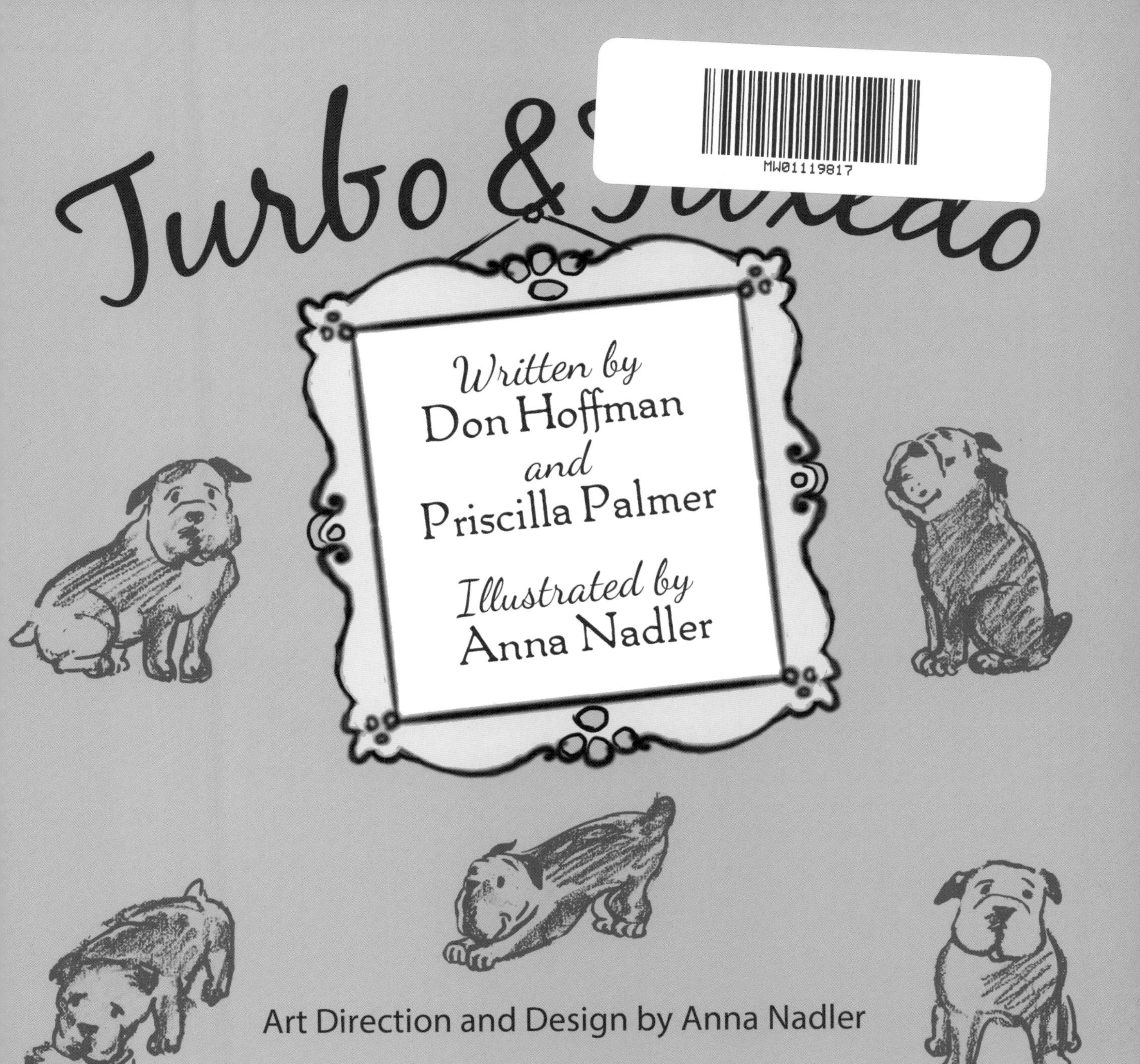

Turbo &
Written by
Don Hoffman
and
Priscilla Palmer
Illustrated by
Anna Nadler
Art Direction and Design by Anna Nadler

Story and Text by Don Hoffman and Priscilla Palmer
Illustrations and Book Design by Anna Nadler

www.turboandtuxedo.com • www.peekaboopublishing.com

Rainbowkidz Publishing
Part of the Peek-A-Boo Publishing Group

First Edition 2016 • Printed by Shenzhen TianHong Printing Co., Ltd. in Shenzhen, China

ISBN: 978-1-943154-27-2 (Hardback)
ISBN: 978-1-943154-04-3 (Paperback)
ISBN: 978-1-943154-13-5 (eBook)
ISBN: 978-1-943154-12-8 (PDF)
ISBN: 978-1-943154-14-2 (Mobi Pocket)

10 9 8 7 6 5 4 3 2 1

On a fine day in *May*, Turbo walked from his house to the park for the first time. The smell of freshly cut grass and yellow daisies tickled his soft puppy nose.

PARK

One sunny day in *June*, Turbo hopped and skipped to the café for breakfast. On the way, he heard a bark in the park.

4

On a warm day in *July*, Turbo stood in the shade to watch the parade. He heard horns and drums. He listened for that special bark.

One sleepy hot day in *August*, Turbo barely noticed the ducks swimming in the pond. He closed his eyes and dreamed of finding a friend.

On a breezy day in *September*,
Turbo chased leaves on the sidewalk.
He pretended they were crispy biscuits.

4

One cool night in *October*, a big harvest moon and millions of stars sparkled in the sky. Turbo lifted his head to stare in wonder.

On a foggy day in *November*,
Turbo tip-toed slowly through the
gray mist. His fur was damp.
He shivered. He felt so alone.

One frosty day in *December*, Turbo sat by the window and gazed out at the frozen park.

On a snowy day in *January*, Turbo jumped into a pile of snow along the path. He hoped for a new friend to play with in the New Year.

One icy day in *February*, Turbo slipped and almost fell on the cold sidewalk. He wished for a warm spring.

On a windy day in *March*, Turbo tossed his head from side to side. Was a friend nearby? He barked again and again.

One rainy day in April, Turbo tripped under the umbrella.
"Excuse me
I didn't see you there."
"Oops! Pardon me!"

Hi! I'm Turbo."
"I'm Tuxedo."
I've been looking for you
very day. I remembered your bark."
"I've been looking for you, too."

On a happy day in *May*, Turbo joined Tuxedo on a walk to the park. They had each found a friend.

Turbo , the best friend in the entire world!
You will forever be in my heart and my memories.
- D.H.